FOR KEiR AND MEiHSiEN

First U.S. edition 1992

First published in Great Britain in 1992 by
Walker Books Ltd., London.

ISBN 1-56402-089-4

Library of Congress Catalog Card Number 91-58764
Library of Congress Cataloging-in-Publication
information is available.

10 9 8 7 6 5 4 3 2 1

Printed in Hong Kong

The artwork in this book is a combination
of marker line drawings and mechanical tints.

Candlewick Press
2067 Massachusetts Avenue
Cambridge, Massachusetts 02140

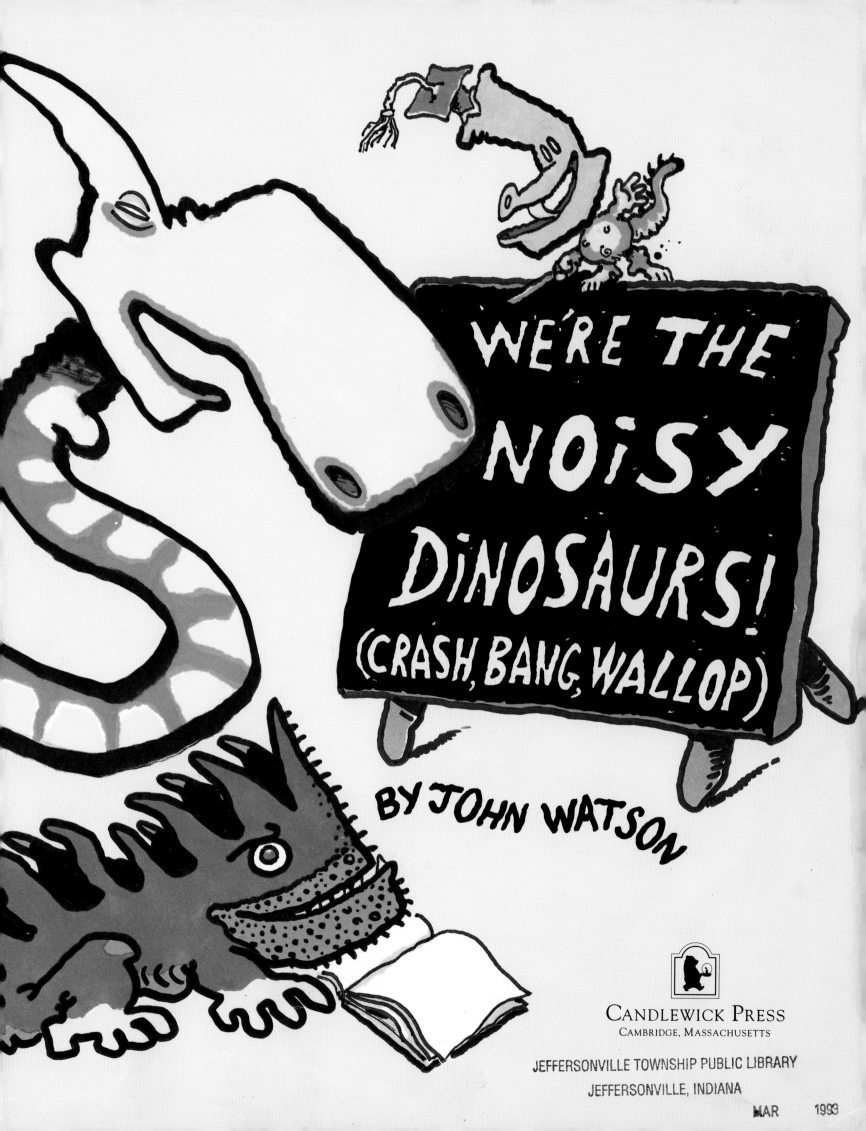

WE'RE THE NOiSY DiNOSAURS! (CRASH, BANG, WALLOP)

BY JOHN WATSON

CANDLEWICK PRESS

CAMBRIDGE, MASSACHUSETTS

IF YOU'RE SLEEPING, WE'LL WAKE YOU UP!
WE'RE THE NOISY DINOSAURS, CRASH, BANG, WALLOP!

WE'RE THE HUNGRY DINOSAURS, UM, UM, UM!
WE'RE THE HUNGRY DINOSAURS, UM, UM, UM!

WE WANT EGGS WITH JAM ON TOP!
WE'RE THE HUNGRY DINOSAURS, UM, UM, UM!

WE'RE THE BUSY DINOSAURS, PLAY, PLAY, PLAY!
WE'RE THE BUSY DINOSAURS, PLAY, PLAY, PLAY!

WE'VE GOT TOYS TO SHARE WITH YOU!
WE'RE THE BUSY DINOSAURS, PLAY, PLAY, PLAY!

WE'RE THE HAPPY DINOSAURS, HA, HA, HA!
WE'RE THE HAPPY DINOSAURS, HA, HA, HA!

WE TELL JOKES AND TICKLE EACH OTHER!
WE'RE THE HAPPY DINOSAURS, HA, HA, HA!

WE'RE THE DANCING DINOSAURS, QUICK, QUICK, SLOW!
WE'RE THE DANCING DINOSAURS, QUICK, QUICK, SLOW!

HOLD OUR HANDS BUT DON'T STEP ON OUR FEET!
WE'RE THE DANCING DINOSAURS, QUICK, QUICK, SLOW!

WE'RE THE THIRSTY DINOSAURS, SLURP, SLURP, GLUG!
WE'RE THE THIRSTY DINOSAURS, SLURP, SLURP, GLUG!

WE'LL DRINK THE SEA AND YOUR BATHWATER TOO!
WE'RE THE THIRSTY DINOSAURS, SLURP, SLURP, GLUG!

WE'RE THE ANGRY DINOSAURS, ROAR, ROAR, ROAR!
WE'RE THE ANGRY DINOSAURS, ROAR, ROAR, ROAR!

GET OUT OF OUR WAY OR WE'LL EAT YOU UP!
WE'RE THE ANGRY DINOSAURS, ROAR, ROAR, ROAR!

WE'RE THE NAUGHTY DINOSAURS, BAD, BAD, BAD!
WE'RE THE NAUGHTY DINOSAURS, BAD, BAD, BAD!

WE SAY SORRY AND PROMISE TO BE GOOD!
WE'RE THE NAUGHTY DINOSAURS, BAD, BAD, BAD!

WE'RE THE QUIET DINOSAURS, SHH, SHH, SSH!
WE'RE THE QUIET DINOSAURS, SHH, SHH, SHH!

WE READ BOOKS AND PLAY HIDE-AND-SEEK!
WE'RE THE QUIET DINOSAURS, SHH, SHH, SHH!

WE'RE THE DIRTY DINOSAURS, SCRUB, SCRUB, SCRUB!
WE'RE THE DIRTY DINOSAURS, SCRUB, SCRUB, SCRUB!

WE WASH OUR NECKS AND BRUSH OUR TEETH!
WE'RE THE DIRTY DINOSAURS, SCRUB, SCRUB, SCRUB!

WE'RE THE SLEEPY DINOSAURS, YAWN, YAWN, YAWN!
WE'RE THE SLEEPY DINOSAURS, YAWN, YAWN, YAWN!

SEND US TO BED WITH A GREAT BIG KISS!
WE'RE THE SLEEPY DINOSAURS, YAWN, YAWN, YAWN!

WE'RE THE DREAMING DINOSAURS, SNORE, SNORE, SNORE!
WE'RE THE DREAMING DINOSAURS, SNORE, SNORE, SNORE!

WE DREAM OF MONSTERS AND CHILDREN TOO!
WE'RE THE DREAMING DINOSAURS, SNORE, SNORE, SNORE!